Getting Rid of Edna

Frieda Hughes was born on the 1st of April 1960, since when
she has led a varied life. Now at the age of 27, she has
written her first novel, *Getting Rid of Edna*. Frieda Hughes
has numerous plans for other books and at present attends
St Martin's and The Central School of Art in London.

Frieda Hughes

Getting Rid of
Edna

Illustrations by Scoular Anderson

Young Piper
Piccolo Books

For Olwyn

First published 1986 by William Heinemann Ltd
This Young Piper edition published 1988 by Pan Books Ltd,
Cavaye Place, London SW10 9PG
9 8 7 6 5 4 3 2 1

© Frieda Hughes 1986
Illustrations © Scoular Anderson 1986

ISBN 0 330 29850 X

Printed in Great Britain by
Richard Clay Ltd, Bungay, Suffolk

Contents

1

Getting Rid of Edna

Miranda climbed out of bed on Monday morning feeling much more light-hearted than she had all weekend. After all, Aunt Edna was going home today. Miranda and Aunt Agatha had taken as much as they could from Edna. She had moved in for the weekend and spent most of her time eating and sleeping, and when she wasn't doing that, she was cooking up spells.

Edna was Aunt Agatha's eldest sister. Miranda's mother had been her youngest, but she had disappeared in a shipwreck before she could pass her magic on to Miranda, who now lived with her Aunt Agatha permanently.

It was Edna's experimental spells that were so hard to put up with. Miranda spent most of her time trying to find out what had been what, before Edna changed it into something else. Even the cats, Andrew and Mona, had not escaped. It took them several hours to find a vacant mousehole to hide in, after Edna tried to shrink them out of existence, but didn't quite succeed and left them the size of mice.

This morning, Aunt Agatha had restored the cats to normal and disposed of some snow and a ski-lift that had appeared in the hall after one of Edna's spells. Feeling quite exhausted, she then headed for the still-room under the stairs to find some vitamin tablets, leaving Miranda to make the best of things as they were.

The kitchen now had a double bed in it so Edna could lie down as she ate straight from the stove. It was a large four-poster, with yards of billowing curtains that always seemed to blow into the soup.

The bathroom sported wall to wall weeds that sprouted through the cracks in the walls and from the pattern on the carpet. There were thistles, dandelions, hogweed, elephant grasses, brambles, dog-daisies, cow parsley and an occasional rose bush. This was all the result of Edna wanting to add a few potted plants to give the bathroom that 'jungle look'.

Miranda could have put up with having an overgrown wash basin to clean her teeth in, but the cows' heads on the cow parsley kept sticking out their tongues at her and trying to suck her fingers like calves do, and the hog-weed grunted at her a lot. She often used the elephant trunks that stuck out from the elephant grass to hold her towel when she had a bath. The dog-daisies were endearing; they had little puppy faces and whimpered at her. The real problem was that, although all these things had roots in the floor and walls, the ones with heads needed feeding as if they were animals.

Miranda was sweeping the hall when she heard strange noises coming from the kitchen. She followed the gurgling sound. Aunt Edna lay on the double bed, waving her hands in the direction of the kitchen window. Miranda ran to the window to see what was outside.

In the yard Aunt Agatha's chickens were trying to eat their corn, but each one had a large worm knotted around its beak. None of them could eat a thing. Edna went on gurgling to herself in amusement.

"Oh, Aunt Edna," cried Miranda, "how could you do such a thing? You have no thought for their feelings!"

Edna looked at her. "But my dear," she said calmly, "they were making the most disturbing noises. I couldn't hear myself well enough to make breakfast."

"You know you only have to snap your fingers to get whatever you want," replied Miranda.

"That's all very well, but things keep going wrong, especially when I'm distracted, and I'm ever so hungry." Edna rubbed her tummy as it growled.

"Haven't you eaten then?" asked Miranda.

"I was just about to when you came in. You can join me if you really want to."

Miranda wasn't too sure about this. Edna's magic was always such a disaster that Miranda had cooked most of the meals herself, the old-fashioned way. Edna waved a hand towards the stove where there was a large plate covered by a silver dome, keeping warm on a low heat. Miranda lifted the lid carefully; underneath was an enormous roast chicken.

"Aunt Edna!" Miranda exclaimed, "you've cooked Percy!"

"Well, it was easier to put a spell on one of those noisy creatures outside, than to cook something out of mid-air," said Edna matter-of-factly.

"You made a mistake," said Miranda with satisfaction. "When you snapped your fingers, you forgot to ask for the feathers to be taken off."

Edna craned her neck to see the top of the stove. Sure enough, Percy the prize chicken was sitting comfortably on a plate in roasted glory, with a full set of beautiful feathers, surrounded by pork sausages.

"Well," said Edna, "I can always try again, can't I?"

"Oh, no you cannot," said Miranda, lifting Percy's remains from the cooker. "I'll take Percy to Aunt Agatha and see if she can do anything, in which case, it's lucky the feathers are still there. Aunt Agatha hasn't quite discovered hair-restorer yet. In the meantime, I will cook you an omelette. And you have Percy to thank for that. She lays most of the eggs."

Aunt Agatha was still in the cellar where she was spending more and more of her time. She was trying to keep out of the way of her sister who was proving a real strain on her usual patience.

As Miranda negotiated the stairs to the cellar, carrying a cup of tea for her aunt and the plate full of Percy, she heard Agatha mumbling to herself. There was a large table against one wall which Aunt Agatha had covered with books. She was reading aloud from one of them.

She looked up as she noticed Miranda. "Was Edna still there when you left her?" she asked. Miranda nodded silently. "Humff, that last spell didn't work then."

"Aunt Agatha," Miranda began, "look what she did to Percy. The rest of the chickens are trussed up with worms, the animal heads in the bathroom are eating so much that their roots are strong enough to crack the walls, and the dandelions have already put three or four feet through the ceiling of the still-room. Aunt Edna has got to go," she finished.

Aunt Agatha sighed. "I must admit the woman is a menace; we ought to fence her off and put 'keep out' signs around her! And she seems to have taken the house over. What's worse, she told me last night that she liked it here so much she thought she would stay for a bit longer."

"No!" cried Miranda, "she's been spoiling everything she touches, and you can't even tell her about her mistakes because she pretends not to hear."

Aunt Agatha looked despairingly at Percy and muttered something under her breath. Percy clucked and shook her feathers. Pork sausages flew everywhere as she leapt off the table and started eating them as quickly as she could. She was starving. The last sausage slid down Percy's beak before she looked up at Miranda and Aunt Agatha with

13

gratitude. Then with a loud squawk, Percy laid two large eggs.

Miranda picked them up and shook them. Then she laughed. "They're hard boiled," she said.

Miranda was busy untying the chickens in the garden. As she was doing this, she noticed that the cherry tree was covered in heavy blossom. But the flowers were pale blue plastic.

"Ugh!" Miranda cried as she picked one of the petals and dropped it.

She untied the last of the hungry chickens and stormed back into the house to find Aunt Agatha again. She was asleep in the cellar and when Miranda shook her to try and wake her, she wouldn't budge. Miranda shook her again, but Aunt Agatha just wouldn't wake up. Miranda was beginning to get really worried. She ran upstairs to the kitchen where Aunt Edna still lay on the bed.

"Aunt Edna," said Miranda firmly, "have you done something to Aunt Agatha?"

Aunt Edna looked at Miranda and said as sweetly as possible, "Why dear, not really.

14

All I did was change the brew that you took her this morning into something that would make her sleep.''

"What ever for?" Miranda asked.

"I had a feeling she was trying to get rid of me, so I took a little precaution in case I was right. I'd rather she slept until I get this place the way I want it.''

Miranda was horrified. It sounded as though Aunt Edna was planning to make her visit a permanent one. "Wake Aunt Agatha up at once!" demanded Miranda, trying to stop feeling frightened.

Aunt Edna was definitely becoming nasty in her old age. She turned to Miranda. "I'll do nothing of the sort. I have no wish to hurt my sister, but why on earth should she have things so easy. I'm the one who's getting old, and I have decided that with you to run the occasional errand, I would be very comfortable here. My magic is getting rusty, and, as you can see, I need careful attention. I'm not as strong as I used to be.'' Edna swept her hand gracefully through the air to indicate that she was talking about her present position on the bed.

"Well, it's a pity that the only spell you've got right had to be the one that put Aunt Agatha to sleep," retorted Miranda.

"Watch your step young lady, or I may get a few spells wrong on you!" said Aunt Edna spitefully.

"But Aunt Edna, you can't just move into someone's house and start changing everything, without even asking permission." But Aunt Edna wasn't listening. She had turned away and gone back to sleep.

Miranda sat in the garden under the plastic-flowered cherry tree, trying to think of a way to get rid of Edna. The pet donkey, Esmeralda, was squatting cross-legged beside the pool, combing her beautiful long hair and using the water as a mirror. This gave Miranda an idea of how to outwit Aunt Edna.

She walked over to the donkey. "Esmeralda," she asked, "where did you get all that lovely hair?"

"I woke up this morning," replied the donkey, "and there it was. I think your visiting aunt found my normal appearance offensive."

"Esmeralda!" cried Miranda. "I asked you a question, but I didn't expect an answer. You're not supposed to talk."

Esmeralda looked sheepish, which wasn't too difficult with all that hair. "Actually," she said, "I quite like being able to talk. The problem is that none of the other animals understands me."

"Yes, I can see that would be a problem," said Miranda thoughtfully, as she watched Esmeralda's reflection in the pool.

"Esmeralda, I have to go now, all right? You don't want anything do you?"

Esmeralda grinned and showed a large row of donkey teeth. "Can I join you for lunch?" she said.

Miranda took down every mirror in the house. The one in the bathroom was difficult because the dandelions were vain little creatures and used it a lot. To get past them she gave them a snack from the larder.

The mirror on the landing was a large one

with a gold-painted frame of carved wooden snakes. Today, because of Edna, the snakes were alive. Miranda decided she had taken enough nonsense for one day, walked up to the mirror and tied all the long necks together in a large knot. The snakes wriggled and squirmed but could not get free.

One by one, Miranda moved all the mirrors to the still-room where her Aunt Agatha normally cooked up her spells. She hung them up until the walls were covered. Then she went to wake Aunt Edna.

"Aunt Edna," she cried, "there is something you really must come and see!"

"What must I see?" asked Edna sleepily. "I want food. I'm hungry."

"In the still-room, it's really strange. I was hoping that with all your knowledge you might be able to tell me what it is," Miranda replied.

"Oh, so there's something you don't know. I'm glad you came to me; I am, after all, an experienced witch," Edna said in a pleased voice.

In the still-room Edna realised there was nothing to see but an enormous number of mirrors. She looked into one of them and patted her huge stomach with satisfaction. "I'm still a fine figure of a woman, even at my age," she said. "Now, what did you bring me to see?"

"Oh, I just wanted to play a trick on you, like you've played on all those poor animals," said Miranda as calmly as possible. "There's nothing to see."

"Really!" shouted Edna. "That is no way to speak to a blood relative; I'll put a stop to this!"

"I wish you would," said Miranda, "those animals have had to change their entire life styles because of what you have done. Especially the donkey."

"Donkey!" shrieked Edna. "I'll turn you into a donkey!" She waved her hands madly in the air.

Miranda ducked, and the spell bounced off the mirror behind her. It hit Aunt Edna. Everything went quiet. Even the snakes around the landing mirror were too busy watching to wriggle any more.

Miranda got up slowly. Edna was standing beside her, sporting a pair of floppy ears, four hooves and a tail. Aunt Edna had become a donkey.

"Look girl! Look what you have made me do!" Big tears rolled down Edna's cheeks. "I can't even turn myself back. A donkey doesn't have any magic!"

Aunt Agatha opened the door and looked at Miranda and Edna in amazement. "Well, Miranda, you seem to have solved the problem. I woke up a few minutes ago to find Esmeralda in the kitchen, asking about an invitation to lunch."

"Sister dear," cried Edna, "help me!"

"Why should I? You put me to sleep and would have left me to sleep for ever, if it had suited you," Aunt Agatha replied. "Since you're so keen to live here, you can live here on my terms. You stay as you are. Miranda, there will be two extra for lunch. And Edna, if you should choose to drive us crazy with your chatter, I will muzzle you!"

2

Spider and the Cat Crash Couch

Andrew and Mona were purring around Miranda's feet as she cooked a special vegetarian lunch for Edna and Esmeralda, the two talking donkeys.

"You haven't told me about all those other things that you cast spells on, Aunt Edna," said Miranda as she stirred lentils into the straw stew.

Edna sat on her haunches on a low stool next to Esmeralda. Her front hooves were on the table. "Why should I?" she replied. "You and Agatha won't turn me back into a witch, so I shall keep my mouth shut!"

"It's a pity you don't keep your mouth shut more often," complained Esmeralda.

Miranda dolloped the soup into a pair of

very deep soup bowls. "Well, Esmeralda, if she talks too much, you must tell me, and I'll put her muzzle on. Then she'll have to listen to you."

Edna's long furry ears drooped at this and she sulked. Andrew slithered under the table and rubbed against Edna's legs; Edna only restrained an impulse to kick the cat because Miranda was watching.

Suddenly, there was a crying at the back door. "Can I come in, please, can I come in? It's so cold out here. Please open the door."

Miranda dumped the soup unceremoniously on the table in front of the donkeys and went to the door. There was no one there. Miranda walked out into the yard, but she still couldn't see anyone.

"I'm down here," said a tiny little voice behind her. Miranda turned to look. Curling its tail around the doorpost was one of the tiniest cats that Miranda had ever seen. It was black, with scattered hairs of ginger. It had long, slim legs and tiny paws, a delicate little pointed face and huge ears.

"Who are you?" asked Miranda.

"I'm a familiar failure," came the reply.

"What's that?" said Miranda curiously.

"Well," started the tiny cat, "you know that most witches have a familiar, usually in the shape of a cat?"

"Yes," said Miranda, "Aunt Agatha has two, Andrew and Mona."

"I'm a familiar too, I was bought as a kitten by a witch who kept treading on me and kicking me when I answered back. She couldn't stand a familiar who talked. So I am a failure."

"Anyway, a few days ago she disappeared, which was all very well, but now I need a new home," said the cat sadly.

"You can join us for something to eat if you like," said Miranda. "You look as though you could do with a good meal. We're just having a normal family lunch."

The cat looked through the kitchen door. "Is that normal?" it asked, looking up at Miranda with its big, black eyes.

Miranda laughed. "It used to be just Aunt Agatha and myself, but the donkeys had an accident and now form part of the family."

"Could your Aunt do with another cat?"

asked the visitor as it meandered gracefully up to the kitchen table.

Andrew looked at Mona. Mona looked at Andrew. 'I don't want competition,' thought Andrew to Mona. 'Neither do I,' thought Mona to Andrew. Miranda didn't know what was going on, because Aunt Agatha's cats couldn't talk. Like most animals, they thought to each other.

Edna was staring at the tiny cat by her feet as though she had seen a ghost. "Brat!" she screamed. "Get out of my sight!" and she pulled her hooves off the floor and tucked them up by her belly.

"Aunt Edna," said Miranda in surprise, "what's the matter?"

The tiny cat mewed prettily. "That's the woman who used to beat me when I spoke," it said.

Miranda stared at Edna in disgust. "You didn't, did you?" she asked. Edna looked ruffled, her ears twitched nervously and she stared into her soup.

"It kept trying to tell me what to do," she muttered.

"That was probably because everything

you did was such a disaster, if your visit here was anything to go by," said Miranda.

Miranda left the animals to their own devices, and went to find Aunt Agatha in the cellar. She had her head in her hands and was staring with intense interest at the table.

"Is anything wrong?" asked Miranda.

"I've made a list of everything we need from the carrier when he calls at the end of the week," said Aunt Agatha, "but there are a lot of new ingredients that would make life much easier. I could get by without them, but they would be very labour-saving."

"Why don't you order some then?" asked Miranda.

"I have no idea what they are, and even if I did, I would need more up-to-date recipe books," replied Aunt Agatha. There was nothing Miranda could say to this, so she asked about the new cat.

"It's only a little thing. It wouldn't take much looking after," she said pleadingly.

Aunt Agatha thought for a bit. Then she said, "Andrew and Mona would have to accept the little cat, before we could give it a permanent home. Besides, it sounds as though this cat of yours has quite a mind of its own."

"I think it wants to stay," Miranda said obstinately. "I know! It could be *my* familiar."

"But you're not a witch," Aunt Agatha reminded her.

"Maybe not, but if anything should happen to you, your magic would pass on to me as I'm your niece and you have no children."

"Cheerful, aren't you?" said Aunt Agatha. "But it's true, you would take my place. All right, if my two accept it, you can keep it. Now leave me to work."

Miranda ran upstairs to break the news to the little cat. It was delighted. "I don't mind not belonging to a real witch, after all I am a failure," it said. "About the only thing I'm good at is remembering facts and figures."

"Like what?" asked Miranda.

"Oh, spell ingredients, price lists, *Financial Times Index*, multiplication tables, *Complete Oxford Dictionary*, the odds on an extra-terrestrial becoming the next prime minister, the population of Australia and so on," replied the cat.

Andrew and Mona sat staring at each other over a bowl of milk, and the donkeys were stunned into silence as Miranda rushed over to the little cat, scooped it into her arms, and ran down to the cellar with it. "Aunt Agatha, Aunt Agatha," she cried, "I think the new cat can solve your problem!"

"Please don't interrupt," Aunt Agatha said impatiently. "I've just got as far as toad spots, lizard feet and frozen beefburgers."

The little cat looked thoughtful. "Frozen beefburgers are out of date, you know," it told them. "If you want to use them in a spell for changing the weather, which is all they're good for, it's much better to use tinned beefburgers, they contain more preservatives, and save using a lot of expensive ingredients."

Aunt Agatha looked at the cat in surprise. "Miranda didn't tell me that you were so well informed. What are you called?"

"A pocket calculator," said the little cat. "If you want a detailed price list of the latest spell ingredients, I have a copy."

The cat leapt out of Miranda's arms and

onto the floor. Then it did a very strange thing. It sat on its haunches and started to unzip little hidden pockets in its fur. Finally, it opened a pocket underneath its left armpit and pulled out a sheaf of paper that you wouldn't have thought for one moment would fit into such a small space.

"Here it is. Nobody has ever wanted my information; Edna thought she knew it all, so I'm a bit rusty as to what is in which pocket." The little cat handed the paper to Aunt Agatha who studied it closely, giving cries of delight and surprise.

Miranda looked down at the pocket calculator. "Well, you've got Aunt Agatha on your side. All you have to do now is win over Andrew and Mona. But keep away from Edna. She and Esmeralda normally only come in for meals but she is bound to be spiteful."

"Oh, I shall be careful," said the little cat. "I've had a lot of practice!"

"What shall I call you then?" asked Miranda. "I can't really call you Familiar Failure or Pocket Calculator. How about Spider?"

"Why Spider?" asked Spider, nibbling a dainty paw.

"Because you are so tiny and about the same colour. But much prettier of course," replied Miranda.

Spider agreed that it did seem appropriate. Then, twitching one of its outsize ears, the cat trotted upstairs to the kitchen, saying, "I'm off to find Andrew and Mona."

Edna was in the middle of telling Esmeralda just what she thought of people taking advantage of Miranda's and Aunt Agatha's hospitality. Esmeralda was telling Edna that she should eat her soup as it was stone cold and her conversation was less than interesting. Andrew and Mona were sitting quietly under the table trying to decide how to get rid of the new cat. But Mona wasn't so keen any more.

'We can't tell it to go,' thought Andrew to Mona, 'because it's supposed to belong to Miranda now. But if there are three of us, there will not be enough attention and food to go around. The little cat should go back to Edna.'

'Andrew, you are cruel,' thought Mona. 'Edna is so unpleasant, and she can hardly look after a cat now that she's a donkey.'

It was at this point that Spider trotted into the kitchen with her tail in the air. She walked daintily across the floor until she reached Andrew. She was only a third his size, but it didn't worry her. She began to purr loudly, and rub against him. Andrew's face went bright red under his white fur. He coughed nervously, and edged away. Spider kept purring and rubbing against him. Andrew stuck his hairy tail straight into the air and pranced out of the room.

'Where is Andrew going?' thought Spider to Mona with curiosity.

'Andrew? He's gone to have a lie down in about the only room in the house that wasn't re-decorated by Edna, before she became a donkey,' replied Mona, 'on the cat-crash couch in the drawing-room.'

'How come that escaped my old mistress? Usually she wrecks everything,' thought Spider. 'She simply cannot remember her spells and they are out of date anyway.'

'She didn't know it existed. Miranda didn't tell her about any of the rooms that weren't in everyday use, and Edna was too lazy to look. Mind you, one or two odd spells slipped under the doors here and there, but nothing serious.' Mona got to her four feet and stretched the middle of her back as high as it would go. 'Come on then,' she thought, 'do you want to see?'

Spider tip-toed after Mona's large, matronly backside as it waddled down the hall to the drawing-room. She swung around the corner with all the grace of a loaf on legs and disappeared through the doorway. Spider peered around the door.

The drawing-room was the most normal room in the house, and usually kept for visitors. Spider noticed there was a patch around the door where a stray spell had obviously seeped through and soaked into the carpet. The carpet was pale blue, but around the doorway it was striped with green and orange, quite horrible.

'Why is your bed called the cat-crash couch,' thought Spider loudly. Mona looked at her, then she pointed a tubby paw at a shelf above the big sofa at the side of the room. Andrew was crouching on it. Suddenly he leapt into mid-air and crash landed amid piles of cushions and a fur blanket on the couch.

'Actually,' confided Mona, 'it's only called the cat-crash couch because we spend most of our time crashed out on it. Andrew is just showing off.'

The three cats were curled up together on the sofa when Miranda came in to make sure they were all right. They looked so sweet and comfortable. What she didn't see, was Andrew's back legs sneaking under his sleeping sister until they reached Spider. Then, ever so gently, he pushed Spider off the edge of the sofa, which wasn't difficult because Spider's silky fur slid anywhere easily.

Spider landed with a wallop on the floor. She looked up at Andrew who was pretending to be asleep, and Mona who really was asleep. Never mind, she had expected some trouble. Carefully she picked up her tail in one paw and leapt back onto the couch.

Pretending she didn't know what had happened, she snuggled really close to Andrew. His long fur wrapped around her and he could hardly move. Andrew got even more annoyed.

When Miranda called the cats to feed them that night, they all trooped into the kitchen to find an enormous bowl of milk waiting for them. Even Andrew was surprised at the size of it. Mona looked at him and smiled; at least he couldn't complain that there wouldn't be enough to go around.

But Andrew wasn't put off. He was still drinking the milk long after Spider and Mona were full. Finally, the bowl was empty. 'I'm still hungry,' he thought to Mona, 'I told you that there wouldn't be enough for us all if she stayed!'

Spider stared at Andrew's stomach, it was huge. He looked like a sack of dried peas with his little back legs almost completely flattened by the weight. But Spider wasn't going to give Andrew room for complaint. Slowly she searched the feet under the table until she found Miranda's. Then she leapt onto Miranda's lap.

"Spider, what is it?" asked Miranda.

"Andrew is still hungry," said Spider politely, "there's no milk left."

"Oh, I'm sorry, I'll give you some more." Miranda filled the bowl with milk again.

Andrew was amazed. He began to realise how useful Spider could be as a translator, whenever he or Mona needed to ask for anything. But he stared at the milk in dismay. Mona was growling at him to drink it, after all, he had said that he was still hungry.

Slowly, lap by lap, Andrew drank the new bowl of milk while Mona and Spider watched, trying not to laugh. Andrew sat by the side of the bowl feeling sick. 'I want to lie down,' he gurgled.

'Come on, Spider, let's get him to the couch,' thought Mona.

Mona took hold of one of Andrew's front paws and Spider took the other, and between them they dragged him to the couch in the drawing-room, and then up onto it. Andrew lay there gasping for breath and trying to look over the huge mass of his belly.

'That will teach you a lesson, won't it,'

thought Mona with amusement. Andrew just stared. He wanted to get angry but didn't feel well enough.

'I'll tell you what,' thought Spider, 'I'll rub your tummy, that will make you feel better.' Andrew was willing to agree to anything.

By the time Aunt Agatha looked in, she found Spider rubbing Andrew's stomach and making strange little cat noises as she told Andrew all about the kinds of things that she could ask the humans for him. Mona was curled up on one of the large cushions, making more strange noises as she laughed every time Spider mentioned food in the conversation, because it made Andrew groan. Aunt Agatha smiled. It seemed they liked each other.

Andrew lay there blowing milk bubbles and decided it was not worth the effort to try to get rid of Spider. Besides, who else had ever offered to rub his tummy?

3

The Acro-Bats

The attic was being cleaned out. Aunt Agatha was having a whale of a time finding all kinds of things she had forgotten about.

"Miranda, look at this. I wore this dress at Cinderella's ball. I was the most beautiful young thing there until Cinderella arrived and outshone us all." Aunt Agatha was holding up a dress that seemed to be see-through and made up of little bits of light sewn together.

"The trouble was," continued Aunt Agatha, "my cousin Beatrice had a soft spot for ill-treated people and had given Cinderella a new dress for the ball. Beatrice had a better dressmaker than I did."

Miranda was digging out more old trunks from between the rafters and blowing the dust off them, before pushing them to Aunt Agatha who had the keys. Miranda would have loved to wear some of the clothes that had been hidden for so long, but with only the chickens and a couple of donkeys with bad taste in clothes to see her, it wasn't really worth it.

One of the trunks was full of old ingredients for strange spells. "You know," said Aunt Agatha, "it might be interesting to try some of these old recipes. I had to use a fairly old one to get rid of the snow and the ski-lift."

Their voices had disturbed the bats who began to complain loudly about the light being on. Miranda looked above her head. The attic was full of long, low beams, and one of the beams at the end of the attic seemed to be wriggling with a life all its own.

The bats had been in the house as long as Aunt Agatha could remember. They came from a long line of talking bats, and were more like large furry mice with big, black wings, than the ordinary kind of bat. When they flew about, their wings took up a lot of room, so they had an arrangement with

Aunt Agatha that the attic was all theirs and they were allowed to use the house on Saturday nights.

Gilbert, the largest bat, flopped across the attic and draped himself on the beam above Miranda's head.

"Miranda," said Gilbert in a sleepy voice, "I thought that the attic was ours."

"But Gilbert, you know we come up here every now and then to bring things up or to take things down. You've never complained before," said Miranda, puzzled.

"Oh, I know that, and I know it's Aunt Agatha's house but we are so tired these days, we really need our rest," said Gilbert. He suddenly did a double backward somersault, a jack-knife and a loop-the-loop and landed back on the beam.

"You see what I mean?" he said despondently.

"Yes," replied Miranda, "but you don't have to do tricks if you don't want to, or are you all training for something?"

Aunt Agatha put down the box she was holding and came to have a look at Gilbert.

"You're not ill?" she asked.

"Nothing like that," Gilbert replied. At that moment, three of the bats on the beam at the end of the attic did a beautifully timed sky dive onto the floor, where they leap-frogged over each other and then flew back to their perch.

"It's awful," Gilbert said as he did a back-flip, "we just can't stop; it's like some kind of disease. We can't sleep for more than five minutes at a time. We're always waking up to do another trick!" Big tears rolled down the fur on his face and off the end of his nose.

Aunt Agatha looked at Miranda. "Go and ask what spell Edna used on these poor creatures. I have to know before I can reverse it."

"Oh, we'd be ever so grateful," cried Gilbert, doing a simple somersault followed by a loop-the-loop backwards.

Miranda found Aunt Edna at the bottom of the garden, sulking. Esmeralda had succeeded in putting her muzzle on and was enjoying a long conversation without any interruptions.

"Hello, Esmeralda," said Miranda, "is

41

Edna behaving herself?'' Edna looked at Miranda in disgust and mumbled something through the muzzle. Miranda unbuckled the muzzle from Edna's nose. ''Edna,'' she said, ''we have to know what it was you did to the bats.''

''What for? They're all right as they are,'' replied Edna. ''I only turned their antics in the attic into something more constructive.'' She twiddled the tip of one of her ears and chewed the tip of the other absent-mindedly.

''You might have asked them first. Surely you can see how exhausting it is for them to have to do tricks all the time! You must tell me what spell you used,'' Miranda said.

''Not telling,'' said Edna shortly.

''Edna,'' Esmeralda piped in, ''if you don't tell Miranda what she wants to know, I will tell you the entire history of my family tree with a full record of their intelligence.''

Edna turned pale beneath her long ears. ''Can't remember,'' she said quietly.

''Are you telling the truth?'' asked Miranda.

''Believe me, she is,'' said Esmeralda with

some satisfaction. "She would never willingly listen to my family history if she could avoid it! Now could you muzzle her again, I would like to finish our conversation."

Miranda returned to Aunt Agatha in the attic with the news. "But I've an idea," Miranda told Aunt Agatha, "we could see if the antidote is in one of these cases. Edna's spells are old, so are the ingredients up here. We could ask Spider if she has a record of Edna's spells for us to work from."

Aunt Agatha smiled at Miranda. It was a good idea. Spider was called. The tiny cat was very cautious as she crept into the attic. The bats were as big as she was and she didn't have the advantage of wings.

"Gilbert," said Miranda, "this is the pocket calculator; her name is Spider."

"Looks like a cat to me," said Gilbert grumpily as he did a little pirouette on one claw while still holding onto the beam.

Spider sat on her haunches and stared up, face-to-face with her first bat. "You're big, aren't you," said Spider carefully.

"We eat creatures your size," said Gilbert.

"Now Gilbert," Miranda cried, "don't be

so rude, you'll frighten her, and she is really the only hope you have!"

Gilbert became very apologetic. "I'll tell you what," he said, "if you can help us, I will give you a personal guided tour of the house and garden."

"What's so special about that?" asked Spider.

"You'll be riding on my back."

Spider quite liked the idea of learning what it was like to fly. And Gilbert's opinion of Spider went up considerably as Spider sat there undoing all her pockets to find a record of Edna's spells.

"She doesn't double up as a sieve, does she?" he asked Miranda. "She seems to have so many holes in her I'm surprised her fur holds together."

Spider was sitting like a kangaroo, looking into a pouch in her belly. She reached one paw right to the bottom of it and gave a sigh of relief. "Here's what I'm looking for," said Spider, pulling out a small package. Aunt Agatha opened it up. It was a very large piece of paper, folded many times into a small, fat bundle.

"There isn't a lot on here," said Aunt Agatha in surprise.

"Well, she didn't know a lot," said Spider. "She used to mix two or three spells together sometimes, to create different results."

"And did it?" asked Miranda.

"You must be joking," Spider purred, "if she wanted fish and chips she could end up with a live shark and a box of matches."

Aunt Agatha was searching through the document for spells to make things acrobatic. Finally she found one for changing people into trapeze artists. "This must be it!" cried Aunt Agatha.

"Can you cure it? Does it have any side effects?" Gilbert asked in desperation, as the bats at the end of the attic attached themselves to each other to form two lines hanging from the beam, then started to swing, while the bats holding the beam turned around and around. This was making them hopelessly dizzy. Little noises of bats trying not to be sick floated through the air.

Aunt Agatha unhooked Gilbert from above Miranda and collected the other bats before they fell. Miranda picked up Spider

and selected some of the old ingredients from one of the trunks. Then they all trooped down to the still-room.

Aunt Agatha piled the bats in a crumpled heap in the corner. They hardly had enough energy to do more than an occasional back-flip. Then she dashed to and fro between the potions that lined the walls, the potions from the attic and the little cauldrons that bubbled in the fireplace, and every now and then, she would reach over to the table to read the piece of paper Spider had produced. Miranda watched Aunt Agatha silently and Spider watched the bats in fascination.

"At last!" cried Aunt Agatha. "I think I've got it. An anti-acrobatics potion!"

Spider backed away as Gilbert separated himself from the other bats and flopped across the floor on his great wings.

"Let *me* try it," he said. "Then if it goes wrong you'll have a chance to try again before the others take it."

Gilbert took a large gulp from the brown, steamy liquid in the pot that Aunt Agatha had put on the floor.

Then he just sat there.

And sat there.

And sat there.

Spider walked around Gilbert cautiously. Then she prodded him in the back with a paw. Gilbert wobbled but otherwise didn't move. Then suddenly he gave a tremendous snore and Spider shot across the room and disappeared behind Miranda's ankles.

Gilbert just kept snoring. "Oh, drat!' exclaimed Aunt Agatha. "Got it wrong, but at least the poor creature will get some sleep now. I'll keep trying. It isn't easy to work out the cure for such an out of date spell; it's a question of trial and error, even for me."

Aunt Agatha concocted a different antidote for each of the bats, then waited to see if any of them would recover.

Three hours later, one bat was green and looked rather like a toad with wings, another was swimming in one of the cauldrons over the fire, others continued to suffer from their acrobatics and Gilbert was still asleep. There was just one small bat who wasn't doing anything, not even sleeping.

The little bat dragged himself across the floor to Aunt Agatha. "Hello," he said, "I'm

Bertram, and I think I'm cured." Bertram flew up to the ceiling and hung from one of the feet belonging to a dandelion in the bathroom. "I feel great! Not even the twinge of a somersault or the pang of a back-flip!"

One by one, Miranda administered the successful antidote to the other bats with a teaspoon. She hated to disturb Gilbert because he looked so peaceful, but then she found that he still wouldn't wake up. Miranda called Aunt Agatha to have a look at him.

"We could always leave him until it wears off, but then he would be fully refreshed and doing so many acrobatics that it is doubtful we could catch him," Aunt Agatha said.

Spider was having a quick search through more of her pockets and then produced an eye-dropper. "Perhaps you could use this?" she suggested.

"Spider!" Miranda cried, "I thought you were only a pocket calculator."

"Well, it seemed stupid to have all this room and not use it," Spider replied.

Miranda administered the antidote to Gilbert with the eye-dropper and then left him to recover. Gilbert soon woke up and thanked Spider, Miranda and Aunt Agatha over and over again.

"When will you be able to take me for a ride on your back?" cried Spider excitedly.

Gilbert took Spider by the paw. "How about now?" he said.

Miranda lifted Spider onto Gilbert's back while the others watched with interest, but Gilbert was flattened by the weight. "Spider," Miranda asked, "what else do you have in your pockets? You are rather heavier than you look."

Spider looked guiltily at the almost unnoticeable bulges in her pockets. She sat up on Gilbert's back and asked him to tell her when she was light enough for him to carry. Out of one pocket came a screw-driver, half a pound of apples that Spider said were for midnight snacks, a manual on how to repair washing machines, a pot of pink gloss paint, a pair of nail clippers and a desk-top diary. Out of another pocket came a two-pound bag of frozen peas and a pea-shooter, the *Complete Works of William Shakespeare* which Spider said she liked to read in her spare time, a packet of Christmas cards and a stuffed parrot.

By this time, Gilbert said he was beginning to notice the difference in weight, and when Spider emptied another pocket of a bag of marbles, a tube of toothpaste, a pack of playing cards and a spare tin of catfood, Gilbert took off at great speed. He flew around the room and out of the window, carrying Spider on her first real flight, with the other bats in hot pursuit.

4

The Carrier Calls

With help from the lists of new ingredients that Spider had produced, Aunt Agatha had finally finished the shopping list for the carrier. He only came around once a year, so everything had to be right.

Miranda was tied to the kitchen again. The donkeys seemed to think they could ask her to feed them any time they felt like it, so she was cooking to stock up the larder. Suddenly there was a loud banging at the back door and a hoarse voice called out. Miranda opened the door and found the carrier standing outside.

He was a short, wizened, old man with more wrinkles than a dried apricot, who spent his whole life travelling from witch to witch, swapping potions for them, and making deliveries to and from the original witches' workshop in Alaska. He was always full of stories from other parts of the world and usually stayed for a few hours, while he ate and drank and told tales to anyone who would listen.

"Hello, Miranda, may I come in?" he croaked. Then, without waiting for a reply, he dragged the sack he had carried on his back through the door.

Miranda busied herself with making some tea and shifting all the barrels and tins she had filled for the donkeys into the larder. The old man made himself comfortable by the stove in one of the wooden armchairs that Miranda and Aunt Agatha used. He put his feet up on his sack as it lay on the floor and let out a great sigh of contentment.

Aunt Agatha came in from the cellar carrying her lists. "Hello, Jim!" she cried with obvious pleasure. "I'm glad you're here. It'll be nice to hear a little of what is going on in the rest of the world!"

Miranda covered the table with biscuits and cakes and a two-gallon tea pot, and sat down with Aunt Agatha to hear what Jim had to say about Aunt Agatha's friends and relations. Jim couldn't resist telling them first about Edna's last order. He still found it difficult to believe that anyone could be so out of date.

"So, what was on the list?" asked Aunt Agatha with curiosity.

"Oh, things like Henry VIII's beard trimmings, a pint of Dracula's cooking sherry, rats' ashes from the fire of London, feathers from the legendary phoenix, which was all very well, but I can never catch the stupid bird these days, after it emerges from one fire it heads straight into another."

"Gracious!" cried Aunt Agatha in amazement. "The poor woman was more backward than we thought. No wonder she kept getting things wrong. Mind you, she is getting on a bit."

"How old is she?" Miranda asked Aunt Agatha.

"I think she was seven hundred and ninety-three on her last birthday," she replied.

"How long ago was that?" Miranda asked.

"About sixty years ago. She stopped counting after that." Aunt Agatha paused for a moment to think of someone else she wanted to ask Jim about.

"What has happened to Griselda lately?" she said at last.

"The Russians have sent her out to Siberia on a mission, but they only gave her a one way ticket. She caused so much trouble that they had to put her into exile," said Jim. "Now she has to use all her powers to keep warm; her list was three thousand tons of spruce firs and a box of firelighters. I shall collect that lot from a gentleman in Africa. She wants to do a swap with him. He'll be getting twenty-seven thousand tons of snow and an ice pack!"

"Does it really all fit in your sack?" asked Miranda, so Jim then insisted that she have a look if she didn't believe it.

He opened the laces that held the sack together and Miranda peered in. She found that she could see piles of miscellaneous objects, from cigarette lighters to voodoo masks, and from lizard tails to frozen beefburgers. There was everything. Then, as her eyes grew accustomed to the dark, she found she could make out the piles of earth that Jim used to keep everything fresh, covered with mountains of snow. There was a freezing wind and a wolf howling somewhere in the distance.

Miranda lifted her head again. Her nose was bright red with the cold. "You have a wolf in there," she told Jim.

Jim peered in himself. "Well I'm darned if you aren't right," he said. "Never mind, there is a witch in South America who would like him. She needs a familiar and would rather have a wolf than a cat."

Aunt Agatha then asked Jim about Beatrice. Jim's eyes filled with what looked suspiciously like tears. "Beatrice," he said wistfully, "beautiful Beatrice."

"Beautiful!" cried Aunt Agatha. "She is the ugliest sister I have. She has a heart of gold but she's still ugly."

Jim moaned. "Your sister Edna, visited her one day for advice and wanted to say thank you. So Edna cast a spell that she thought would be good for Beatrice and asked that Beatrice become as beautiful as her heart. Beatrice did become as beautiful as her heart, but all in solid gold."

Aunt Agatha was scandalised and threatened to have Edna turned into a donkey of stone. When she had calmed down, she searched the pockets of her skirts until she found the tiny bottle she was looking for, and handed it to Jim. "You'll be visiting Beatrice in about two weeks. Rub this all over the gold and it should bring her back to life." Jim thanked Aunt Agatha and pocketed the bottle with a sigh. He finished off the last of the Black Forest gateau and said that he had to be getting along.

"But before I forget," he said, "there are one or two things for you, Agatha."

He opened his sack again. Besides Aunt Agatha's last order, there were some presents. There was half a pound of moon dust from Aunt Agatha's cousin at Cape Canaveral, six ounces of eucalyptus leaves from a supernatural koala bear in Barbados, a stuffed pike from an admirer in Devon, a box of jumping beans from a sister in Mexico, and a set of ready-heated, sky-blue hair rollers from a witch in South America.

Aunt Agatha surveyed her gifts. It felt almost like Christmas. "Send the stuffed pike to my brother on Lake Victoria with my compliments," she said firmly. "I've nowhere to put it and he's a fisherman. The rest I will keep." Then Aunt Agatha gave Jim her order of ingredients for his next visit, and her gifts for other witches.

"Just one thing, before I go," said Jim suddenly, "there is a little gift for Miranda." Miranda was delighted. She watched closely as Jim fished around in his sack again.

His hand emerged, holding something that wriggled furiously. "It's been a bit of a problem, really," said Jim. "Your cousin, Demelza sent it. She breeds them." As he held out the creature to Miranda, it slipped from his grasp and half slithered half ran to the door.

It was gone before anyone could catch it. "It's all right," said Jim, shrugging his shoulders, "it'll make straight for the fishpond and stay there. Now I must be off." He shouldered his sack and disappeared down the garden path.

The cats followed Miranda as she went to

search the fish pond for her present.

'It's a fish,' thought Andrew.

'It's a cat,' thought Mona.

'I have a nasty feeling that you're both right!' thought Spider.

Sitting in the pool, with its elbows on the bank, was a little cat, but the half of it in the water was not cat but a fish tail.

"Hi, everybody!" it said. The cats looked at each other then looked back at the cat, or the fish, or the both.

Spider didn't hesitate, she whipped a notepad out of one of her pockets. "Right," she said, licking the tip of her felt pen to make it work better.

"What do you think you're doing?" Miranda cried.

"I'm taking down details. I mean, apart from other things, I have to record it as the first talking catfish."

"Now, what's your name?" Spider asked the creature.

"Tomas," said the top end of the creature.

"No, Frederick," said the bottom end.

"It might solve your problem to split the names in half," suggested Miranda.

"The top half of me is Tomas," explained the creature, "and the bottom half is Frederick. I would agree if I could be called Tomerick because Tomas comes first."

"What are you?" asked Spider.

"A mercat," said the mercat, "as in mermaid, at least, that's what I call my-self."

"Perhaps you could tell us why there seem to be two of you in the same animal," said Spider as she put away her notebook in despair.

"Two of me? Ha! there aren't two of me at all!" laughed the mercat, "but the top of me has to have a voice and so has the bottom half. If the bottom half of me went for a swim it might drown the top half. If the top half of me stayed in the sun too long, the bottom half of me might die. They both have to have a say for their own good."

The mercat hauled itself onto the bank of the pool, and shook itself. It really was half cat and half fish. Andrew's eyes bulged at the sight of all that fish! Miranda was beginning to wish that she hadn't got up that morning. She left the three and a half cats and half a fish to amuse themselves while she went to find Aunt Agatha.

Miranda and Aunt Agatha were sitting in the kitchen sipping endless cups of tea and trying to decide what to do about Tomerick, when the donkeys sauntered in, asking for their toasted teacakes and clotted cream.

"Did you know," said Esmeralda, "that there are three and a half cats in the garden, all squabbling over who should eat the half fish."

Miranda leapt to her feet. "But they can't eat it!" she cried. "The mercat will die without his tail!"

"Well, I would do something about it now," said Aunt Edna disagreeably, twitching her donkey ears towards the smell of burning teacakes on the stove.

Miranda ran into the garden to find that Andrew had hold of Tomerick's tail in his mouth. He had dug his fat backside into the ground to stop Mona from pulling him over. Mona had hold of the mercat under the arms and Spider was holding onto Mona's waist.

Andrew was snarling, his greed had definitely got the better of him. Tomerick was suspended in mid-air between them, and was howling his head off.

Before Miranda could reach the cats, Tomerick had split in half, leaving his tail in Andrew's mouth. Mona screamed a little cat scream, and Spider just sat there, horrified. The mercat was definitely in two pieces.

Miranda was furious, she stormed up to a cowering Andrew and pulled the fish's tail out of his mouth, then she took the top half of the mercat from Mona. As she did this, out of the top half of the mercat dropped a tiny kitten, giggling with merriment as though it found the whole thing a great joke, and out of the bottom half dropped a small fish with the most beautiful blue and green colouring that Miranda had ever seen. The two little creatures ignored all the staring faces and crawled towards each other.

"Hello, Tomas," said the fish, "I always wondered what you would look like with back legs. They suit you!"

"And I always wondered what you would look like," said Tomas. "At least you won't have to live on my rats and mice any more!"

The two of them shook paw and flipper. "Well, Frederick," said Tomas, "I hope that you will understand, but the climate around here isn't very healthy for you and I will have to put you back in the pool for safe-keeping." Tomas looked accusingly at Andrew who backed away.

Then Tomas picked Frederick up by his dorsal fin, ever so gently, and carried him to the pool where he let the fish go. The kitten turned as smartly on its heel as a small fur puff-ball possibly could and trotted back to Miranda.

"Well," it said, "even I didn't think this was possible!"

Miranda was speechless. She was still thinking of a practical answer to the new problems that another cat would produce, when Mona answered the question for her. Mona picked the kitten up by the scruff of the neck, unzipped one of Spider's front pockets and dropped the kitten into the pouch like a baby kangaroo. Then the two cats trotted off to the house with their tails and their noses high in the air, totally ignoring Andrew. They had made up their own minds to keep the mercat.

5

The Grimster

Aunt Agatha was working in the still-room at her favourite pastime: sorting out cupboards. There were two tables, full of bottles and jars. As each container came out of a cupboard or off a shelf, she looked at the label and put it carefully on one table or the other.

Miranda was curious as usual. She examined the bottles and jars on one of the tables. There was moon dust, mushroom juice, frogs' feet, camels' whiskers, powdered garden gnomes, dried anchovies, a tin of tomato soup and many other strange things.

Miranda gathered that this was the table for ingredients still in current use. The other table was a little different. There was everything from dried squirrel ears, a pint of water from Mount Vesuvius, and a hamster's tail, to hairs from Merlin's donkey, snakes preserved in sugar-water, and a bottle of tomato soup from the First World War. Many other bottles and jars were so old that the labels had faded completely.

"What are you going to be doing with all these old ingredients?" Miranda asked Aunt Agatha. Aunt Agatha smiled.

"I can't bear to throw them away. I shall use them all up today."

"What, all at once?" Miranda asked. Aunt Agatha nodded.

Finally, all the cupboards and shelves were empty and Aunt Agatha polished the surfaces before putting back all the things she wanted to keep. Then she sent Miranda to fetch a large mirror.

The mirror was put in the middle of the floor and Aunt Agatha sprinkled a mixture of fine powders in a small heap in the centre. She added a few small feathers, followed by the snakes in the sugar-water and the hamster's tail. Then she carefully stirred in a little of the old tomato soup.

The result was dramatic. A wisp of smoke rose from the squashy heap on the mirror and began to take shape. A huge shape. It was a large animal, the height of Aunt Agatha herself, completely covered with long black fur. It patted its belly with one of the enormous paws that had been hanging by its side. "I've arrived!" he cried in delight, and started to slide his feet to the edge of the mirror.

"Wait," said Aunt Agatha, "you must stay there for a bit longer."

"Why?" asked the big, black thing.

"We don't know what to do with you yet!" Aunt Agatha replied. "After all, I was only using some of my old ingredients to see what would happen."

The creature began to sob and he wiped his runny eyes with his large paws. "Nobody ever wants me. I always seem to end up as an unwanted spell somewhere." The creature's tears were forming a positive puddle, which looked revolting as it mixed with the concoction around its feet. He was a real mess.

"Look," he said, "I can cook and clean, I

can wash dishes, and I only live off scraps. I don't take up very much room; I get on well with other animals and I'm a great draught excluder."

Miranda looked pleadingly at Aunt Agatha. Aunt Agatha felt that they had to do something with the creature. It wasn't fair to make it appear and then tell it they didn't want it. Its feelings would be terribly hurt, and if it kept sobbing, it would rapidly give them a serious damp problem.

"All right," said Aunt Agatha at last. "Miranda really does seem to need help looking after the other animals, and I'm always too busy. If she can teach you to do the housework, I think that we can say we'll keep you. But I also think it would be fair for us to say that if you're not satisfactory you'll have to go."

The monster was so grateful. It leapt off the mirror and covered Aunt Agatha with sloppy kisses. "You can call me Grimster," he said, "after the hamster's tail that you threw in. I'm a Grim Hamster, you see." Grimster laughed at his joke. He did rather resemble a hamster, but was about seventy times the size, with enormous damp eyes that glowed in the dark. Grimster waved to Aunt Agatha as Miranda towed him away to the kitchen.

"No, Grimster," said Miranda yet again, "the dishes are washed after they are used, not thrown away. We don't have an endless supply of plates."

"But most witches do, don't they?" asked Grimster.

"Maybe, but we try to live as normally as possible, besides, it takes a load off Aunt Agatha if she doesn't have to spend all her time wishing up new crockery," replied Miranda.

Grimster opened the dustbin again, and lifted out the plates he had just put in. "Now," said Miranda, "put the dishes in the sink, fill the sink with hot water and add a little soap. *Not* the whole packet either." She leaned over Grimster and just managed to prevent him from emptying an entire month's supply of soap suds down the drain. He had forgotten to put the plug in.

It took Miranda nearly two hours to teach

Grimster to do the washing up. She let him put everything on the draining-board to drip-dry. Next, Miranda started to show Grimster how to dust and generally clean the house. This wasn't easy either. He tucked his fur in with the sheets and got his claws caught in the bedspread. He swept all the dust on the floors into piles beneath the carpets, and then jumped on the lumps to flatten them, so Miranda wouldn't notice. Miranda stopped Grimster, just in time, from rolling up the stair carpet to shake it outside. Miranda had to nail it back in place.

Then there was the bathroom. Grimster disappeared into the bathroom for a long time, and when Miranda came to see how he was getting on, she found him asleep in a bath full of cold water. The plants seemed wary of the intruder and were silent.

"What on earth do you think you are doing?" she cried as she stepped over one of the dandelions. Grimster opened his eyes and blinked.

"Oh, I do apologise," he gurgled as he slipped under the water line. He struggled to

pull himself up until he was in a sitting position.

"You see," he said, "none of the other places where I appeared ever had a bath. Neither did the Grimster Retreat in the Horse Head Nebula where I had to spend most of my time, and you must have noticed that all that muck on your Aunt's mirror got in between my toes and caused me some discomfort."

He lifted a foot out of the water and flexed it to show that under all the fur, he did have toes. Complete with talons. He retracted his claws and lowered his foot back into the bath with a sigh.

"Do you know what I think?" Miranda shouted at him. "I think that you think that we are stupid. And what I really think is that you're lazy. I think that you should think that we might think your laziness was the reason that you kept getting sent back to the Grimster Retreat. That's what I think."

Grimster cowered and began to sob again, but Miranda wasn't going to take any more of his wheedling. "You can get out of that bath this minute, put yourself through the mangle in the yard so that you don't drip all over the house, and get on with what I've been showing you. The day after tomorrow we're having people to tea and I will not have you turning the place into a halfway house for lazy creatures like yourself. I thought that you told us you could clean and cook and do all those other things!"

Grimster looked at Miranda in horror. He had stopped sobbing. "And I thought she was such a nice girl," he mumbled under his breath. Then he said to Miranda, "I lied."

"What on earth for?" Miranda cried. "What was the point?"

"I didn't want to be sent back to the Grimster Retreat. Everyone who has ever made me appear has either done it by mistake, a little like you did, or wanted something else. They thought a Grimster wouldn't mind! Then when I wouldn't do what they wanted, having a mind of my own, they always sent me back where I came from. Besides," he said proudly, "we are noted for being lazy liars."

Miranda scowled at him and he hurried on.

"I would be sitting in limbo, waiting to be wanted, then POOF, and I would be staring at some nut who had been trying to get a pet elephant, or a talking budgie, or even a potted aspidistra or a new tea set. As soon as they came to their senses, off I would trot, back to the Grimster Retreat."

The Grimster stood up in the bath and nearly all the water disappeared, soaking into his fur. He wrung out his beard and the water level rose two inches. "You can send me back now, if you like," he said, as he pulled one of his toes out of the plug-hole.

Miranda thought for a moment. "You don't want to stay then?" she asked.

The Grimster stared at her. "I would simply love to stay," he said, "but you don't want a Grimster that is not only lazy but tells lies as well, do you?" He couldn't help sounding hopeful.

"If you would promise not to lie, and really to do some of the work around the house like you told us you could, I will let you stay. Now that I know you have never done it before, I won't expect miracles, but I will expect you not to be so lazy."

"It's a deal, it's a deal!" cried the Grimster, jumping up and down and denting the bottom of the bath.

"Right," said Miranda, "if you get outside and put yourself through the mangle, and then try and get some work done, I won't even mention it to Aunt Agatha."

Grimster lifted the heavy fur around his legs like a skirt, leapt over a dandelion and two hogweeds and shot out of the door, down the stairs and through the mangle.

Aunt Agatha was standing in the hall, and got showered with droplets as Grimster rushed past her at something approaching the speed of light. "What's got into him?" she asked Miranda.

"Oh, I think he thought that he didn't really have a chance of staying, so he didn't try too hard at first. But he'll be much better now. He should be all right to help with Sunday's tea party." Miranda smiled.

6

The Tea Party

One Sunday a month, Aunt Agatha would invite some of her favourite friends and relations to tea. This Sunday was that once-a-month Sunday. As always, the main worry was the possibility of some odd, uninvited guest turning up.

Miranda had finished tidying away one or two things the bats had knocked over during the night, and had locked Esmeralda and Edna in the garden shed to keep them from eating the cakes she was baking.

Back in the kitchen, Andrew, Mona and Tomas had got themselves shut in the larder and were making short work of the donkeys' jelly babies. Spider was sitting on the kitchen table, searching her pockets for recipes that Miranda wanted, while Grimster was busy

77

reading the *Good Housekeeping Guide* Spider had found for him.

Aunt Agatha had retreated to the cellar with a bottle of aspirin. She was suffering from a severe headache brought on by listening to too much of her sister, Edna, at breakfast. She wanted to recover her senses before her guests started arriving that afternoon.

The drawing-room was beginning to fill up with delicious things for the guests to eat. The spare dining table was loaded and so were all the side tables, and Grimster was up to his hairy elbows making up the last lot of cake mix when the first visitor arrived. It was Gertrude, a distant cousin of Aunt Agatha's. Miranda showed her into the kitchen to keep her company until the others arrived.

Miranda had seen photos of Gertrude when she was younger, tall and slim and quite beautiful. She was still tall and slim and quite beautiful, but the photos were black and white and Gertrude was green.

"Hello, darling!" cried Gertrude as she greeted Grimster. "You must be the home help." Grimster growled.

Miranda wondered how she could keep

Gertrude entertained until Aunt Agatha emerged from the cellar. How did anyone make conversation with a green stranger? Did you ask, 'What is it like to be green?' or did you simply say, 'What a lovely colour you are today.' Miranda didn't know where to start. So she asked what the weather had been like on Gertrude's journey. It was a fairly safe question.

"Oh, my dear, the weather was delightful. Instead of doing a simple transportation job to get here, I decided I would like a holiday, so I took the pretty route and stopped in France for a while. I spent most of my time there drinking *crème de menthe*, hence the reaction I had. But I think that green suits me, don't you?"

"You mean that you aren't really green at all?" Miranda asked in astonishment.

"But my dear!" exclaimed Gertrude, "you didn't think that I was green all the time did you?" Miranda blushed and nodded. "Oh, no, sometimes I'm pink, sometimes I'm blue. I vary a lot. You see, I take on the colour of whatever I eat and drink," added Gertrude happily.

By this time the other guests had started arriving. Aunt Agatha had emerged from the cellar to direct everyone to the drawing-room, where Gertrude and Miranda joined them, leaving Grimster to cope with making the several gallons of tea needed, and replenishing the tables when necessary.

Aunt Agatha went round her guests, encouraging them to start eating and generally greeting them all, at the same time she was selling raffle tickets for the witches' retirement home, her favourite charity. Edna was the prize. Edna was to do someone some good at last: she was offered as a four-footed home help for the lucky winner. The party seemed like a happy, family gathering, the sort that most normal people like.

There was Uncle Jack from India, who had arrived in long white robes, chanting to anyone who would listen. Aunt Agatha sat him by the window with a plateful of honey biscuits and three pints of tea, where he would bother as few people as possible.

"Ah, Susannah," cried Aunt Agatha with delight, as she saw someone who was obviously a very old friend. A very, very,

very, very old friend. Susannah was only four feet high and looked about eighty thousand years old.

"Agatha, my dear child," croaked Susannah, "I'm delighted to see you again after so long. I hope you don't mind, but I've parked my dinosaur in the yard."

Miranda looked out of one of the windows, and there, covered in prehistoric dust, was a very tired *tyrannosaurus rex*, looking anything but frightening.

Aunt Agatha's brother Simon was struggling through the crowd with a worried look on his face. "Agatha," he said nervously, "I hope that you don't mind, but I was in the middle of a move from Turkey, when your invitation caught me, and I ended up bringing my family. Can they come in?" he asked.

"Why, of course, I would have invited them if I had only known earlier. Where are they now?" said Aunt Agatha warmly.

"Waiting outside," replied Simon.

"Go and get them then," said Aunt Agatha.

Simon disappeared. A moment later he

was back. "Agatha, I would like to introduce you to some of my family," he said.

Aunt Agatha just stood and stared at the enormous number of ladies, all wearing veils, who had suddenly appeared in her drawing-room. There were twenty of them.

"Who on earth are they all?" she asked.

Simon smiled proudly. "My wives," he said, "my harem."

"I knew you must have had an ulterior motive to go to Turkey in the first place," exclaimed Aunt Agatha. "How did you get them all here?"

"On a magic carpet of course," replied Simon, "actually, it was a flying football field. They didn't have a carpet big enough for us."

"And just where did you put it?" said Aunt Agatha. Simon pointed out of the window and everyone turned to look. At the bottom of the garden just beyond the garden gate, was a football field complete with players and referee.

"Good grief!" cried Aunt Agatha. "I hope that you don't expect me to feed them as well!" Simon put a comforting arm around his sister's shoulders. "Of course not," he said, "their air tickets didn't include meals. I have to drop them off at Wembley Stadium after I leave."

"Well, that's something I suppose," said Aunt Agatha a little ungraciously. She handed each of her brother's wives a plate, and asked them to help themselves. The women proceeded to clear large areas of the food covered tables, and Grimster had to be called from the kitchen with more cakes.

Miranda thought things were going very well. Gertrude was talking to Gilda who also had a problem with food, only instead of changing colour, Gilda got lighter the more food she ate. A loving godmother had put a spell on her when she was a baby, so she never put on weight when she ate a lot.

Gertrude was lying on the sofa staring at the ceiling, where Gilda was bobbing about, having fallen victim to Aunt Agatha's two-ton sponge which was irresistable. Granny-too-good-to-be-true, Aunt Agatha's great, great grandmother, was knitting an extra-large chin warmer for a particularly fat cousin, her long hooked nose and pointed, wrinkled chin sometimes getting in the way of the knitting needles.

Aunt Agatha's brother Jack had become involved with Simon, and was trying to persuade him to give up his wives and become a holy man. The discussion came to an abrupt end when Simon offered one of his wives to Jack, and Jack instantly gave up being a holy man.

Miranda made herself useful by distributing more tea and cakes until she was distracted by another knock on the back door. 'Oh no,' she thought, 'it'll probably be someone we didn't invite and didn't want to come.'

Closing the drawing-room door behind her, Miranda made for the back door in the kitchen and opened it warily.

"Good afternoon," said an educated voice, "I do hope I haven't called at an inconvenient moment, but I am the new vicar in the parish, and I wondered if it would be a good time for me to come and introduce myself."

Miranda stared at him with her mouth open. All she could think about were the people milling around the drawing-room, all weird and not one of them was even a church goer.

Pulling herself together, she smiled. "I hope you will excuse me," she said, "but I live here with my aunt. I will just go and get her. Would you like to sit in the kitchen for a moment. I won't be long."

Miranda walked quietly to the kitchen door, she opened it gently and then closed it behind her. Then she ran along the hall as fast as her legs would carry her and into the drawing-room.

"What's got into you all of a sudden?" asked Aunt Agatha.

"Oh, Aunt Agatha, Aunt Agatha, there is a vicar in the kitchen!"

Suddenly, the whole room went quiet. Agatha stared at Miranda.

"What!" she exclaimed, "a real live vicar?"

"Yes," replied Miranda. "I told him you would go and speak to him, but we can't leave him sitting in the kitchen. They expect

to be offered tea and cakes in the drawing-
room, don't they?"

Aunt Agatha chewed her thumbs for a
moment, trying to think fast. She didn't
want her guests to leave after they had
travelled so far, and the vicar would hear if
she put them all in some other part of the
house. Anyway, there wasn't time.

"We will just have to make things look as
normal as possible," she said finally, "and
invite him to join us."

Agatha eyed her guests and saw few who
looked normal. Enlisting Grimster's help,
Aunt Agatha and Miranda rushed around
the room. They stuffed their friends and
relatives under chairs, behind chairs, up the
chimney and under the carpet. They pushed
Granny-too-good-to-be-true into a cupboard, with her knitting and her outsize
handbag, and hid Susannah under a cushion
on the sofa. Most of the guests seemed to
think it was a party game.

The remaining people could just pass for
normal. Aunt Agatha straightened her skirt,
squared her shoulders and went to greet
their unexpected visitor.

It was only as he heard the voices of Aunt Agatha and the vicar in the corridor, that Grimster realised they had forgotten Gertrude on the settee. With great presence of mind he whipped the cloth off the big table from under the plates and cakes, and spread it over her. As the door opened, he also realised that he did not classify as normal either, and did the first thing that came into his head; he threw himself onto the carpet in front of the fire place.

The door shut. Aunt Agatha, with great politeness, was informing the vicar that it would be a positive pleasure to have him join her guests, and she began to introduce him to the people that were left. Most of these were Simon's wives, looking decorative in their Eastern clothes but otherwise normal.

The vicar chose to sit on the sofa. In fact, he chose to sit on Gertrude who was really brave and didn't make a sound. He had his feet resting on Aunt Agatha's beautiful hearth-rug.

As Miranda poured a cup of tea for the vicar, from the tap on the tea urn, she sincerely hoped that Uncle Jack's feet were

fairly clean. The tea urn had been the only place left to hide him.

"I don't mean to frighten you," said the vicar, making conversation, "but did you know that some of the people in the village still believe that my parish is haunted? Especially this old house. Many of them can't understand how you can live here."

"Oh, Reverend Williams," laughed Aunt Agatha nervously, "I couldn't live anywhere else. This house has been in the family for years. I'm very attached to it."

The vicar took another bite of his meringue pear and swallowed a sugar maggot. "I must say, though," he said, "I find it difficult to believe in ghosts, don't you? And witches as well. I mean, such things are simply figments of the imagination, don't you agree?"

Aunt Agatha just smiled politely and Miranda wondered what would happen if the vicar realised that he was having tea with a figment of his imagination.

Then she suddenly noticed that the effects of the food were wearing off Gilda, and that Gilda was directly above the vicar's head.

Quietly, she got up, picked up a piece of two-ton sponge from the side table and walked behind the sofa. Gilda was definitely sagging, she was only eighteen inches above the vicar by the time Miranda reached her. Miranda handed Gilda the cake and Gilda took some quick mouthfuls that sent her up to the ceiling again.

Miranda sauntered back to her chair, being careful to avoid treading on Grimster. "Ah," said Reverend Williams, "I notice that you have a lovely fur rug!" Miranda went bright red. She hoped the vicar wouldn't examine the rug too closely.

To Aunt Agatha's and Miranda's relief, the vicar changed the subject and told them about his travels. He bored them with his stories for another hour before he decided to leave. He walked all over Grimster on his way out.

As the door closed behind Aunt Agatha and the vicar, Grimster let out an enormous gasp. "I promise," he said, "that I will never walk across another fur rug, just in case it's me!"

Miranda uncovered Gertrude who was

lying with an imprint of the vicar's seat across her knees. "Goodness," said Miranda, "he must have been very uncomfortable, and very polite not to say so!" and at that moment, the last of the cake wore off Gilda completely, who landed with a wallop, in Gertrude's lap.

One by one, Miranda rescued all her aunt's not-so-normal friends and relatives from their hiding places.

Granny-too-good-to-be-true was still knitting, and the other various guests headed for the tea urn for a reviving pint. Jack didn't ever want to see tea again and crawled out of the top of the tea urn looking like a little, brown, drowned rat. He took the wife that Simon had given him and went to sulk in the cupboard that Granny-too-good-to-be-true had just vacated.

Then it was time for the draw. There was a moment's silence as Aunt Agatha picked the winning raffle ticket from a hat, and Simon found he had won Aunt Edna. Miranda had to go and fetch Edna from the garden shed and lead her into the room to present her to Simon.

No one spoke as Miranda handed Simon the donkey's reins. Aunt Edna's face twitched furiously. To Miranda's horror it was obvious she was about to become abusive, but, at that very moment, Simon's wives realised they had a pet. They crowded around Edna, laughing and stroking her, and feeding her biscuits. Edna was loving it! She had the total attention of twenty women, all making a fuss of her. She even condescended to carry three of them to the flying football field, where the footballers were saying goodbye to the dinosaur.

All the visitors stood in the yard as the field took off and soared above their heads. Everyone was too surprised at Aunt Edna's reaction to Simon's wives to speak until she had disappeared over the trees.

Finally, one by one, contented and happy, the guests each made their farewells and left. Miranda and Aunt Agatha knew that this tea party had been a success. They had survived a visit from the vicar, and even found a good home for Edna.

The vicar, incidentally, spent several weeks visiting the local doctor because he swore that he had seen a dinosaur playing football on a football pitch that wasn't there any more.

Betsy Byars
The Not-Just Anybody Family £1.95

It made all the headlines when Vern broke *into* prison, but what would you do if your grandpa was in jail? The Blossoms had no doubts. Since they couldn't get Pap out, Maggie and Vern had to get in. A little unusual, perhaps, but as Maggie said, 'We Blossoms have never been just "anybody".'

This is the first adventure for the Blossoms – Pap, Vern, Maggie, Junior and Mud the dog. They're a family you won't forget.

Rose Tremain
Journey to the Volcano £1.95

'As they swam, their eyes stayed fixed on the volcano. The black cloud sat tight on its rim. Then, up through the black cloud and spurting high into the clear sky above it came a gush of flame, higher than any fountain, brighter than any firework...
  "She's going!" cried Guido.'

Trouble had been brewing all summer, from the day George's mother left his father and snatched George from his London school. Escaping to his mother's old home on the slopes of Mount Etna, George found himself plunged into the heart of a large family he barely knew. Life on the mountain was exciting and different. But under the sunny slopes lay a seething mass of molten lava, waiting to erupt...

All these books are available at your local bookshop or newsagent, or can be ordered direct from the publisher. Indicate the number of copies required and fill in the form below.

Send to: **CS Department, Pan Books Ltd., P.O. Box 40, Basingstoke, Hants. RG21 2YT.**

or phone: 0256 469551 (Ansaphone), quoting title, author and Credit Card number.

Please enclose a remittance* to the value of the cover price plus: 60p for the first book plus 30p per copy for each additional book ordered to a maximum charge of £2.40 to cover postage and packing.

*Payment may be made in sterling by UK personal cheque, postal order, sterling draft or international money order, made payable to Pan Books Ltd.

Alternatively by Barclaycard/Access:

Card No. | | | | | | | | | | | | | | | | | | |

Signature:

Applicable only in the UK and Republic of Ireland.

While every effort is made to keep prices low, it is sometimes necessary to increase prices at short notice. Pan Books reserve the right to show on covers and charge new retail prices which may differ from those advertised in the text or elsewhere.

NAME AND ADDRESS IN BLOCK LETTERS PLEASE:

Name———————————————————————————

Address—————————————————————————

3/87